Always Remember Fairy Dust

Clean Teeth equals

The Tooth Collector Fairies
Batina's Best First Day

Written by: Denise Ditto

Illustrated by: Gabhor Utomo

A Ditto Enterprises Production

The Tooth Collector Fairies
Batina's Best First Day
Text © 2016 by Denise Ditto Satterfield
Illustrations © 2016 by Ditto Enterprises

All rights reserved. No part of this book may be reproduced in any form, by any electronic or mechanical means, including information storage and retrieval systems, without permission in writing from the publisher, except by a reviewer who may quote brief passages in a review.

Requests for permission to make copies of any part of this work should be sent to either address below.
Ditto Enterprises, PO Box 2063, Montgomery, TX 77356 USA
www.toothcollectorfairies.com

First Edition

Book layout and cover design by Ira S. Van Scoyoc
Publishing consultant: Pam Van Scoyoc
Copyedited by Amy Hardwick

Ditto, Denise, author.
    The Tooth Collector Fairies: Batina's best first day / written by Denise Ditto ; illustrated by Gabhor Utomo.
    pages cm
    SUMMARY: In the magical land of Brushelot it is Batina's first day collecting teeth. She is determined that her humongous wings will not interfere with her mission, but on her way back, with the tooth secure in her pouch, her wings cause her to tumble and the tooth is lost. Batina must call on her best friends, Lainey and little Lulu, to work together to save the day.
    Audience: Ages 5-9.
    ISBN 978-0-9967559-1-7

    1. Tooth Fairy (Legendary character)--Juvenile fiction. 2. Fairies--Juvenile fiction. 3. Teeth--Juvenile fiction. [1. Tooth Fairy--Fiction. 2. Fairies--Fiction. 3. Teeth--Fiction.] I. Utomo, Gabhor, illustrator. II. Title. III. Title: Batina's best first day.

PZ7.1.D58To 2015   [E]
                              QBI15-1628

Printed in the USA
Published in the USA

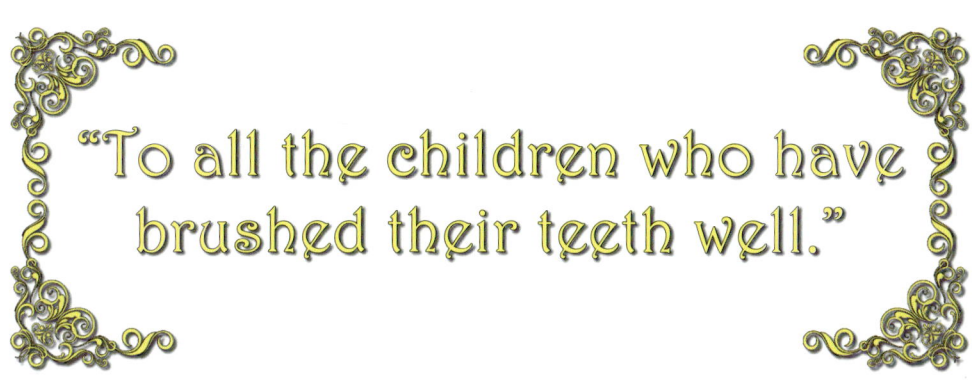
"To all the children who have brushed their teeth well."

Table of Contents

Chapter 1	1
Chapter 2	5
Chapter 3	9
Chapter 4	15
Chapter 5	19
Chapter 6	23
Chapter 7	27
Chapter 8	33
Chapter 9	39

Chapter 1

Batina's eyes fluttered open when a kaleidoscope of pink and orange rays of light danced across the floor into her room. *Ting, ting, ting . . . ting, ting, ting.* She sat up, rubbed her sleepy eyes, looked over at the tooth alarm, and thought, *Someone's lost a tooth!*

She sprung from bed, her sparkly green wings with pink polka dots unfolding like those of a beautiful butterfly. They were spectacular, and they were big. In fact, they were humungous—three times the size of the other fairies' wings in the magical land of Brushelot. Sometimes they made her clumsy, but not today. She was determined to prove they would not interfere with her new job as Tooth Collector. She would be the best collector ever.

To prepare for her flight, Batina jumped into the shower and giggled as she stood under the rain-can shower head and pulled down the drawstring. Rainbow-colored fairy dust, the very dust that enabled her to fly, floated down like snowflakes, tickling her from head to toe.

Perfect, she thought and laughed as she shimmied and shook. *Now I'm ready for my journey.* She folded her wings and headed for the front door.

Outside, a large crowd of Tooth Collectors gathered. Batina spotted Lainey, one of her best friends since birth, standing across the bridge at Milk Fountain. Lainey was the smartest fairy in Brushelot, passing all of the Tooth Collector tests with perfect scores.

Some of the other fairies called her a smarty pants, but not Batina; she was proud to have such an intelligent best friend.

Batina waved and shouted, "Hey, Lainey!" and flew over to join

Chapter 1

her. "Can you believe it? Our first assignment day is finally here."

"I know," Lainey said. "When my alarm went off this morning, it scared me half to death. I rolled right off the bed! It's a good thing I got my cotton-ball carpet replaced yesterday. It was so soft I bounced right back up off the floor."

Batina giggled and said, "It's a good thing you didn't break your glasses."

Looking around at the crowd, Batina said, "Hey, where's Lulu? I wonder if her alarm went off, too."

"I'm down here!" Lulu shouted.

Lulu was the tiniest fairy in Brushelot, standing only four inches tall—one-half the size of Batina.

"Oh, hey, Lulu," Batina said. "Sorry, I didn't see you. Jump up here for a better view." Lulu lightly fluttered her wings and landed gently on Batina's shoulder.

Batina said, "We are so lucky to get assignments on the same day. It looks like a lot of kids lost teeth last night. It's going to be a very busy day."

"I calculate there is approximately ninety-eight percent of our Tooth Collector class gathered here today," Lainey said as she adjusted her glasses. "That could be a record breaker."

Batina laughed and said,

"Thanks, Lainey, for that important information."

All three friends joined hands and awaited the arrival of Crown Mistress Molar, the oldest and wisest Tooth Collector.

Chapter 2

A hush grew over the crowd when Crown Mistress Molar and her assistants arrived. Her purple wings with white stripes fluttered gracefully as she approached the podium to make the departure speech.

She began, saying, "Welcome, Tooth Collectors. It is your mission to collect lost teeth and return them safely to Brushelot. Upon return, the teeth will be inspected. All well-brushed teeth will be selected to undergo a magical transformation—a transformation that will turn them into fairy dust. As you know, in order to fly, we need fairy dust."

She paused and turned toward her staff. With the flip of her hand, she ordered them to begin passing out the Tooth Collectors' assignments. Turning back to the crowd,

she continued. "Let nothing stand in your way to complete your mission! Is everyone ready?"

The crowd cheered in agreement.

"Very well," Crown Mistress Molar said. "Be careful on your journey, and bring your teeth home safely. For those of you on your first assignment, please return here tonight for the awards ceremony, where one of you will receive the Best First Day ribbon. Until then, good luck and good day!"

Crown Mistress Molar stepped back from the microphone, waved farewell to the crowd, and took to the air.

Batina quivered. "Did you hear that? There's going to be a ribbon awarded to someone for having the best first day! That could be one of us!"

"I know," Lainey said. "Unfortunately, the odds of winning are slim, considering the number of tooth fairies collecting teeth today."

Batina smiled. "Don't be so negative, Lainey. It's possible."

Before takeoff, all the Tooth Collector fairies joined hands to chant aloud the motto from *The Tooth Collector Handbook*. It was tradition, and Batina was the loudest. "Clean teeth make fairy dust, the very dust that enables us to fly! Clean teeth make fairy dust, the very dust that enables us to fly!"

Someone yelled out, "Hey look, everyone! It's Batina and her rabble of misfits."

Chapter 2

Batina turned to see Jolene, the local bully, leaning against the lamppost on the corner of Pearl Drive and Floss Street. Her orange wings were hard to miss. Her wild, blue hair was piled on top of her head in a bun with toothpicks sticking out everywhere. *Only crazy Jolene would wear toothpicks in her hair*, she thought.

"Don't look now, but it's jealous Jolene."

Sneaking a quick peek over her shoulder, Lainey asked, "Why is she so mean? It's not our fault she didn't make the collection team. She should have studied."

"Right," Batina said. "Let's just focus on our mission and forget about her."

The starting whistle blew, and the Tooth Collectors took off like rockets—that is, except for Batina. Her wings got caught in the strong draft, and she spiraled down to the ground, landing with a thump.

Pointing and shouting, Jolene said, "Ha, ha, ha! There she goes again—already messing up, and on her first day. Hey, Batina, face it: you'll never be a good Tooth Collector."

Ignoring Jolene, Batina jumped up, shook her wings, and tried again. This time she soared high into the pink and orange skies of

Brushelot until she was out of sight.

In a flash, she was at the home of a child who had lost a tooth. She cautiously entered the house, careful not

to knock anything down. Hovering behind the bedroom curtain, she calmed her fluttering wings and waited to make sure the child was asleep.

She flew to his bedside and gently reached under the pillow. "Ah ha—here it is," she whispered, holding up the tooth in the moonlight. She smiled and thought, *This looks like a very-well-brushed tooth. What a fine job this boy has done brushing his teeth!*

She placed a surprise under his pillow, tucked the tooth carefully in her pouch, and hurried back to Brushelot to have the tooth inspected.

Chapter 3

The front door of the Tooth Inspection Department flew open with a bang. In tumbled Batina, skidding to a halt right on the large feet of Mr. Gizmo, the Tooth

Inspector.

"Batina, what happened to you?" he asked, jumping back.

She leapt up, untangled her wings, and said, "Nothing, Mr. Gizmo. Just a little turbulence. No problem. I'm okay—I'm okay."

"Well, I'm glad you're okay. That was quite a landing," he said as he walked back to his desk. "And you're back so quickly after your late start. In fact, you're the first fairy to return."

Batina beamed with joy. "These wings may be awkward, but with them I can fly faster than a bee."

"I see that," Mr. Gizmo said, scratching his beard. "Do you have something for me?"

"Yes, I do," Batina replied proudly, reaching into her pouch. "Oh, no!" she cried.

"What's wrong?"

Batina turned her pouch inside out and shook it. "Where's my tooth?" she asked. "See, look—it's gone. What could have happened to it? I know I put it right here. I know I did." Frantically, she turned to search the room for her lost tooth, looking under tables and chairs and behind baskets and doors, but it was nowhere to be found. "What am I going to do?" she cried out. "I can't fail my first mission!"

"Keep looking, my dear," Mr. Gizmo said calmly. "I'm sure you'll find it."

Batina continued her search as other Tooth Collectors arrived with teeth for Mr. Gizmo's inspection. Lulu and Lainey soon returned, and Batina rushed to them. Stammering to avoid crying, she said, "Thank g-goodness you're here."

"What's the matter?" Lulu asked.

Batina tried to explain. "Wh-when I la-landed, I w-was caught in a-another strong br-breeze and I lost my b-balance and my f-first tooth."

"Oh, no!" they both said together.

"It has to be here somewhere," Lainey said. "C'mon—we'll help you look for it."

Together the three friends began searching, looking under tables and chairs and behind baskets and doors again.

Mr. Gizmo completed his inspection of all of the collected teeth—except for Batina's. He turned to her and said, "I'm sorry, Batina, but it's time to send the well-brushed teeth on to Dominic in the Manufacturing Department."

"Wait!" Lulu hollered, squeezing herself out of a crack

in the floor next to Mr. Gizmo's briefcase. "I think I found it! I think I found it!" She held out the tooth to Batina. "Is this it?"

Batina squealed with delight. "Yes, that's it, Lulu! That's it. Thank you so much for finding it! I don't know what I'd do without you."

Fluttering her wings happily and beaming with pride, Batina turned to Mr. Gizmo. "Here's my tooth," she said as she handed it to him for inspection.

"Yes, indeed," Mr. Gizmo said. "Here it is." He placed it on his desk and sat back down. He clicked on his overhead lamp, opened the top drawer, and picked up the tweezers with his chubby little fingers. Chuckling, he said, "I must be very careful. One lost tooth today is enough."

Mr. Gizmo positioned his magnifying eyeglass back on his round, rosy face and began his final inspection. The tooth glistened in the light as he turned it to and fro. "Hmmm." Batina held her breath as she awaited his approval. "You know, Batina, only well-brushed teeth are selected for transformation into fairy dust," he said. "And this is a well-brushed tooth!"

Batina let out a sigh of relief, and everyone shouted, "Hooray!"

Mr. Gizmo spun around in his chair and placed the tooth onto the conveyor belt behind his desk. "Let's get these teeth to Dominic."

Chapter 4

Mr. Gizmo reached back and flipped the conveyor belt's power switch to ON. Nothing happened. He flipped the switch back and forth again, but still nothing. Puzzled, he looked at Batina and her friends and said, "What could be wrong with the conveyor belt? This has never happened before."

Rrrrrr, rrrrr, rrrrr . . .

Batina cupped her hand to her ear said, "I can hear the motor running."

Lulu sniffed the air. "Smells like something's burning."

"Maybe there's something wrong with the rollers," Lainey said. "Let's take a look." The fairies flew around the conveyor belt, hoping to discover the problem.

Lulu pointed and let out a shriek. "Look over there! There's something stuck in the rollers."

Batina and Lainey flew around to join Lulu on the other side of the machine.

"What is that?" Batina asked. "It looks like . . . like a toothpick. Wait a minute," she said, trying to keep her cool. She turned to Mr. Gizmo and said, "Was Jolene in here today?"

"No. You know only Tooth Collectors are allowed in the Inspection Department."

"Hmmm. Well, I saw Jolene this morning, and she was wearing toothpicks in her hair. You don't think she could have sneaked in here and tried to sabotage our mission, do you?" Batina asked.

Shaking his head, Mr. Gizmo said, "It's possible, but I would hope not. No one has ever deliberately tried to

Chapter 4

interfere with the magical transformation process. That would be very disappointing."

He went back to his desk and retrieved his tweezers. With his eyepiece in place and a steady hand, Mr. Gizmo plucked the toothpick from the roller. He turned the switch on again, and this time it worked perfectly. The sparkling, well-brushed teeth bounced along on the conveyor belt as they rolled away.

Batina raised her fist in the air in triumph. "Don't worry, Mr. Gizmo—no one can stop us from completing our mission."

Chapter 5

The Manufacturing Department bustled with fairies gathered to watch the well-brushed teeth arrive. Batina had never been in this department before and didn't know what to expect. A humming sound filled the room. She turned to see all the teeth arriving. When they reached the end of the line, they dropped into a very large basket.

When the basket couldn't hold another tooth, Dominic hollered, "Shut off the conveyor belt!"

Wayne, Dominic's assistant, turned the switch to OFF. He bent down, grabbed the basket by the handles, and lifted it up with a grunt. Slowly, careful not to spill any teeth, Wayne carried the basket to Dominic, who was

waiting for him in front of a big, black curtain that hung in the middle of the room.

Dominic bowed and said, "Thank you, Wayne." He then turned toward the fairies. In a loud voice and with an outstretched hand he said, "Welcome, Tooth Collectors, to the Manufacturing Department. This is where the teeth you collected are transformed into fairy dust. As you know, without well-brushed teeth, Tooth Collector fairies could not fly. Today I see we have a full basket. Everyone should be very proud."

The fairies clapped their hands and fluttered their wings.

Dominic raised his hand for silence. Then, without warning, he started whirling around like a spinning top.

Chapter 5

He also wobbled from side to side like a bowl of Jell-O. When he finally stopped, he was facing the black curtain. He balanced himself and straightened his hat. Then he reached into his coat pocket and pulled out a golden whistle. Placing it to his mouth, he blew three short times: *tweet, tweet, tweet*. The room started to buzz. The black curtain rustled and began to open slowly, inch by inch.

When it was fully opened, the fairies let out a loud "AAHHH!" because right there in front of them, behind that curtain, smack dab in the middle of the Manufacturing Department, stood a huge metal box the size of a school bus! It had spouts on both ends and a horn-shaped chimney on top. On the side, painted in very big red, yellow, and blue letters were the words Super-Duper Magic Dust-Making Machine. It was magnificent!

Chapter 6

With basket in hand, Dominic walked over to the Super-Duper Magic Dust-Making Machine. Standing on his tiny tippy toes, he lifted the basket up to the spout. Tilting it, he shook, shook, shook, pouring every last sparkling, well-brushed tooth into the machine.

"This is the moment you've been waiting for," he said as he reached over and flipped the switch to ON. The Super-Duper Magic Dust-Making Machine moaned and groaned. It sputtered and it spat. A large cloud of gray smoke billowed out of the horn-shaped chimney with a toot and lifted high into the air.

"Uh-oh!" Dominic said, and it sputtered and tooted

again. Leaning over, he placed his ear on the side of the machine and listened, then shook his head. "That's not good. We seem to be having some technical difficulties here." He pointed toward the back of the machine. "Can someone please check the plug?"

First-responder Batina raced behind the machine and reported back. "All looks good here, Dominic."

"Okay. Well, let's try again." Still nothing. Scratching his head, he said, "It looks like the machine might be in overload. This has never happened before. We must find a solution to this problem: without the magical transformation of the well-brushed teeth into fairy dust, Tooth Collector fairies will never fly again."

The room filled with the sound of loud talking as everyone shared ideas and discussed options for how to fix the problem.

Batina looked at Lulu and Lainey and said, "I know we can figure this out. Think, fairies, think."

The three fairy friends closed their eyes for a minute to concentrate. Batina's wings began to tremble and twitch, and she shouted, "I've got it! I have an idea. We can switch to fairy power. *The Tooth Collector Handbook* clearly states that in times of emergency, fairy power can be stronger than any power in the land."

Lainey agreed. "You're right, Batina. I don't know why I didn't think of that first."

Dominic said, "Yes, of course. That's what we can do: we can switch to fairy power."

Chapter 6

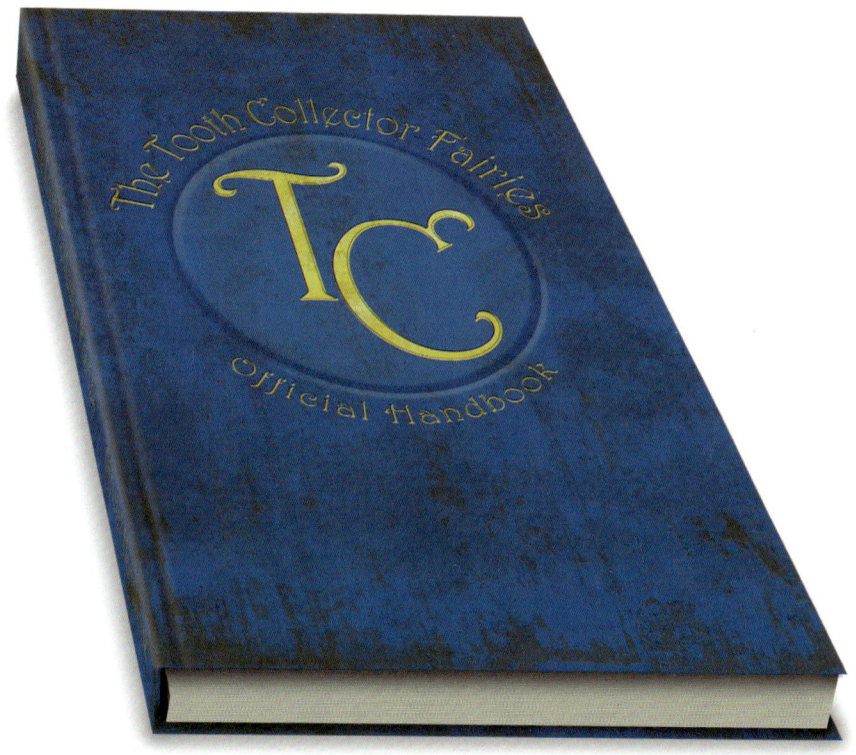

Chapter 7

Determined not to let anyone or anything stop the magical process, Batina took charge. She cried out, "Everyone, gather around and join hands. This is what we are going to do: we are going to build a fairy chain of power."

Grabbing the power cord from the wall, she said, "Take this, Lulu. We'll line up shortest to tallest fairy. "Lulu, you're in front. Everyone else, grab hold. I'll take the back of the line."

All the fairies in the Manufacturing Department joined hands—that is, except for Jolene, who stood in the shadows by the back door, watching. Batina looked up and saw her. "Jolene, that means you, too!

Get over here. We need everyone! C'mon, grab my hand."

With eyes cast down, Jolene slowly crept toward the machine. Batina shouted, "Hurry up!" Jolene smiled sheepishly and then picked up speed, flying to Batina's side, where they joined hands.

"Is everyone ready?" Batina asked.

"Yes!"

"Okay, on the count of three, start flapping. One, two, three: flap!"

All the fairies began flapping. The Super-Duper Magic Dust-Making Machine rumbled and grumbled, lit up for a second, and then stopped.

"One more time," Batina shouted, and their wings flapped and flapped again.

The Super-Duper Magic Dust-Making Machine lit up again and rocked back and forth before grating to a stop.

"This ought to work," Lainey said. "Let's try again." The fairies took three long, deep breaths. This time they all shouted, "One, two, three!" and everyone flapped. They flapped so hard that Dominic had to hold on to his hat!

The Super-Duper Magic Dust-Making Machine lit up, and the black curtains blew. Jolene shouted, "Flap!"

The Super-Duper Magic Dust-Making Machine rocked back and forth. Lainey yelled, "Batina, can you stretch your wings any bigger? We need more wind power."

"I think I can," Batina shouted back. "Hold on!" She shook her wings and stretched them out farther than she had ever stretched them before. "Oh, no. Now I can't reach Jolene's hand."

Lainey looked at Jolene and had an idea. "Take one of those toothpicks out of your hair. We can use it as an extension."

Jolene plucked the longest toothpick she could find

out of her hair. She held one end of the toothpick, and Batina held the other.

"I can reach now! I can reach now!"

Batina shouted with glee. "Okay, everyone ready. On the count of three. One, two, three: FLAP!"

Batina flapped and fluttered so hard that she and Jolene both lifted right off the ground. The room shook,

and there was a loud *BANG!* And, just like that, the Super-Duper Magic Dust-Making Machine started purring like a kitten.

"You've done it; you've done it!" Dominic shouted. "It's working. It's finally working!"

"Hooray!" The fairies all stepped away from the machine, clapping and laughing.

Batina wrapped her fully extended wings around her best friends. "Come here, Jolene," she said and wrapped her up as well. "Thank you so much for your help."

Chapter 8

*C*LANG! Startled, all the fairies jumped back. A large cloud of peppermint-colored smoke billowed out of the chimney, making curly cues in the air. The magical transformation of the well-brushed teeth had begun: This is what everyone had been waiting for. In less than a minute, hundreds of little canisters of rainbow-colored dust came popping out of the machine like popcorn—one for every tooth collected. *Pop, pop, pop. Pop, pop, pop.*

Everyone burst into cheers and joined hands for the fairy-dust dance, including Jolene. With teamwork, all of the shiny, well-brushed teeth completed the journey.

One by one, each Tooth Collector danced over to the machine and picked up a canister of dust. They danced

all the way back to Milk Fountain, where Crown Mistress Molar was waiting to announce the winner of the Best

First Day ribbon. As soon as everyone arrived, Crown Mistress Molar approached the podium. Behind her stood her assistants, Mr. Gizmo, Wayne, Dominic, and the Brushelot Marching Band.

"Tooth Collectors and all fairies in the land of Brushelot, we had a remarkable, record-breaking day. All collected teeth were well-brushed and magically transformed into fairy dust. Everyone, including the children, did a remarkable job. And now, it is time to announce the winner of the Best First Day ribbon."

Batina, Lulu, Lainey, and Jolene stood in the crowd, wings a flutter in anticipation of the decision.

Chapter 8

Crown Mistress Molar continued. "One fairy stood out today. She faced many obstacles, but she persevered. Her determination to get the job done was well noted."

Everyone held their breath; the crowd had never been so quiet. The fairy friends held pinky fingers, their eyes tightly shut.

Crown Mistress Molar went on to say, "The winner of the Best First Day ribbon is . . . Batina!"

The crowd erupted with cheers. The Brushelot Marching Band played the famous winner's song while hundreds of multicolored balloons were released into the air. Batina was speechless. How could she be the winner? She wanted to receive the Best First Day ribbon but thought for sure that with all of her mishaps she would not be selected.

Lainey and Lulu fluttered around Batina. Everyone congratulated her, even Jolene. Batina flew up to the podium to receive her award and make her acceptance speech. The crowd quieted.

"Thank you so much for this award," she said,

fighting back tears of joy and holding up the ribbon. "I will cherish it forever." Batina looked down at her ribbon and then turned to whisper something to Crown Mistress Molar, who smiled in return. Batina turned back to the microphone. "I never could have won this award without the help of my two best friends, so I would like to share it with them. C'mon on up here, Lainey and Lulu. Stand with me. I would also like to give a special thank-you

shout-out to my friend Jolene. Although she is not an official Tooth Collector, she was instrumental in helping us successfully complete our mission today. Thank you, Jolene."

The crowd went crazy. Never in the history of Brushelot had someone shared an award or recognized anyone at the ceremony other than a Tooth Collector.

This was indeed a remarkable best first day.

Chapter 9

After much celebration, the ceremony concluded and the Tooth Collector fairies began to make their way home. Batina saw Jolene standing alone in the corner with her head down. She flew over to her and said, "What's the matter, Jolene?"

Jolene sniffled. "It was me. I tried to sabotage your mission today. I put the toothpick in the conveyor belt. That was a horrible thing to do. I'm sorry, Batina. Can you ever forgive me?"

"I knew it was you, Jolene. I knew it. I mean, after all, you are the only fairy in Brushelot who wears toothpicks in her hair. What were you thinking? I can forgive you, but I sure hope you don't ever try a stunt like that again."

"I won't, Batina. I promise I won't."

Lainey and Lulu walked up just then. "What a great day," Lainey said.

Lulu yawned and said, "I know. It was so much fun."

"It was fun," Batina said, "but it's getting dark, and we all better get home."

Jolene waved goodbye to her new friends as she

walked away. Batina, Lulu, and Lainey didn't walk—they danced all the way home. When they got there, each fairy put a new canister of rainbow-colored dust in her rain-can shower head to replenish her fairy-dust supply.

Before crawling into bed that night, Batina hung her Best First Day ribbon on her bedpost and smiled.